A
FORTUNATE
NAME

By Margaret Mahy:

The Door in the Air and Other Stories

BOOK TWO OF
THE COUSINS QUARTET

A

FORTUNATE
NAME

MARGARET MAHY

ILLUSTRATED BY

MARIAN YOUNG

DELACORTE PRESS

Published by
Delacorte Press
Bantam Doubleday Dell Publishing Group, Inc.
1540 Broadway
New York, New York 10036

A Vanessa Hamilton Book

Text copyright © 1993 by Margaret Mahy
Illustrations copyright © 1993 by Marian Young

Book design by Claire Naylon Vaccaro

Library of Congress Cataloging in Publication Data

Mahy, Margaret.
  A Fortunate name / by Margaret Mahy ; illustrated by Marian Young.
     p.   cm.
  Summary: As the only Bancroft in a family of Fortunes, Lolly has always
felt left out of her Fortune cousins' exclusive gang, but when her parents
separate Lolly discovers a new inner strength and aspects of kinship that go
beyond names.
  ISBN 0-385-31135-4
  [1. Family problems—Fiction. 2. Self-acceptance—Fiction. 3. Cousins
—Fiction. 4. New Zealand—Fiction.] I. Young, Marian, ill. II. Title.
PZ7.M2773Fo 1993
[Fic]—dc20   93-560 CIP AC

Manufactured in the United States of America

November 1993

10   9   8   7   6   5   4   3   2   1

A
FORTUNATE
NAME

CHAPTER 1

From deep in her bed Lolly Bancroft heard the sound of voices arguing. Or perhaps she dreamed them. She heard (or dreamed) the sound of glass breaking. Was it a real fight, or was she hearing voices from a television program? Quick footsteps moved down the hall. She heard an angry, hissing whisper going past her door, but could not make out any words.

Lolly sat up in bed.

"What's wrong?" she called in a voice soft and smudgy with sleep.

The angry, hissing whisper stopped immediately.

"It's all right, Lolly," said her father in a calm voice. "Go to sleep again, there's a good girl."

Lolly lay down again. Now that she knew it was her father outside her door, she felt warm and safe again. Perhaps he had broken something and was cross with himself. Almost at once, she fell asleep again.

When she awoke next, it really *was* morning. The house was completely quiet. Lolly turned over, stretching. Too quiet, she thought suddenly, remembering her dream of angry voices and glass breaking in another room.

First a fierce dream, and now this great silence.

Though a Bancroft morning was never noisy, it was usually filled with polite, gentle sounds. The toaster pinged. The electric kettle purred. Lolly's father, Ivor Bancroft, sorted through his papers— which were never bent and grubby like Lolly's pages of homework. Ivor's papers made silky, self-satisfied, kissing sounds as they touched each other. Not only that, the usual Bancroft morning smelled of bacon and toast. This morning, there were no sounds and no smells. The air was empty.

Lolly scrambled out of bed. The silence made her tiptoe as if she were about to creep up on something dangerous. Out of her room she went, and down the hall. Listening hard, she felt as if her ears were stretching out from the side of her head. She opened the living-room door.

A dim light filtered in through the curtains, which were still drawn. The pale, mouse-gray carpet her father had chosen so carefully gleamed like silver in the early-morning light. There was nobody in the room. There were no kitchen sounds from next door, though the serving hatch was open. Sun, shining through this golden peephole, was like light from another world.

As she tiptoed reverently across the carpet, Lolly felt a sudden, thin pain on the sole of her right foot. Jerking her foot into the air, a drop of blood fell slowly, like a dark tear, leaving a blob on the carpet. The blood was a wonderful color, so dark a red that it looked almost black. Part of Lolly's mind enjoyed the color, even as she stared in horror. She was standing among tiny, glittering daggers of glass. She was bleeding onto the new carpet.

Lolly half expected her father to appear behind her, sighing and shaking his head at her clumsiness. Looking startled and guilty, still holding one foot in the air, she glanced around rapidly and saw that the room had changed since last night. Something was missing. The photograph of her father's

mother, the grandmother who insisted on being known as Honoria because she so hated to be called Grandmother, had disappeared.

As long as Lolly could remember, that picture had stood on the coffee table, pretending to smile sweetly, but secretly sneering at her. Now it had gone. Just as well! Honoria Bancroft would certainly have arched her brows and turned down the corners of her mouth at the blood on the mouse-gray carpet. *She doesn't get that clumsiness from the Bancrofts,* the photograph would have said in its wordless way. Honoria said things like that, speaking over Lolly's head as if Lolly would not be able to hear simply because she was shorter than the adults around her.

There were steps on the outside path and then the click and rattle of the back door opening. The wind chimes hanging in the porch gave out a soft, sweet note. Someone walked through the kitchen. A shadow passed across the golden peephole of the serving hatch. As Lolly stared, the kitchen door opened. Lorna, her mother, came in, wearing yesterday's crumpled clothes, as if she had been up all night. Lolly and her mother stared at one another.

"I've just been for a morning walk," her mother

said in a guilty voice. "Oh, Lolly! What's happened to your foot, darling?"

"I cut it," Lolly whispered, wobbling as she tried to keep her foot in the air. She could feel a beetle of blood crawling over her heel. "What's happened? What's wrong?"

"Nothing," said Lorna, and then she sighed and added, "well, something *is* wrong. I'll put a plaster on your foot and have one cup of coffee, and then I'll tell you all."

"Tell me now," begged Lolly, feeling herself turn pale with horror. Her father had been killed by a burglar! He had been kidnapped by terrorists working for a rival bank! In spite of his sighing and head shaking, Lolly loved her father dearly.

"Lolly, darling," said Lorna, falling to her knees beside Lolly, and flinging her arms around her. "I'm sorry! I'm *so* sorry!"

That settled it. That blood on the mouse-gray carpet which Ivor had chosen must be a sign of his death. It had been his ghost speaking at her door in the night. The room whirled.

"Your father and I have had a major fight. Not just one of those polite little Bancroft ones. A real, hot, Fortune fight. I hit him over the head with his mother's picture and he ran off to her at one o'clock in the morning," Lorna said.

The room still whirled. Her foot still hurt. Lolly felt the safe, solid world around her go all crumbly. At first she was so glad to know that Ivor was still alive that the news was almost a happy surprise. Blood on the carpet was *not* a sign of death, only of divorce. A moment later, the thought of any separation seemed like death of another kind.

"Darling heart!" cried Lorna. "You're my wonderful girl, but all he ever does is to criticize you. And me! The only person he wants to please is his *mother*. I've had twelve years of it. I've had enough."

"Bring him back," Lolly said. "But I'll clean up the carpet first." Her mother hugged her harder.

"Forget the carpet," she cried. "Lolly, it's because of me, not you. Look, I've really tried to be a Bancroft for years and years, but I'm not going to try anymore. Blast the Bancrofts. I'm going back to being a Fortune again . . . and I'm taking you with me."

CHAPTER
2

"You've got to eat more breakfast," Lorna said.

"*You* aren't having anything," Lolly pointed out.

"That's different," Lorna said. "Don't worry me, Lolly. Eat something." Lolly did not want her mother to worry, and so she drank her orange juice and ate some muesli. Lorna hovered and flitted, like a protective fairy, straightening things that were already straight.

At this time in the morning Ivor was usually at work. In a way, everything was as it usually was . . . just Lorna, Lolly, and breakfast. But everything felt odd. Lolly looked down at the tabletop, half expecting to see thin cracks creeping across it, but it was perfectly sound. Perhaps she herself, Lolly Bancroft, was crumbling away. She got up from the table, knocking over the sugar bowl.

"Where are you going?" asked Lorna, hastily rescuing the bowl.

"Out to the swing," said Lolly.

Lolly was a bold swinger, and swung hard and high, feeling like an eagle or a fighter pilot, or Tarzan, or someone taming the wild horses of the air. If only she were allowed to sit on a swing during her classes at St. Joseph's Convent, she felt sure she would always be top of the class.

To her surprise, she found that once she was on the swing, moving backwards and forwards, the crumbling stopped. Perhaps it was because swinging was already full of sudden changes. Dad's run away from home . . . down, down, down. I'm going to be a Fortune, not a Bancroft . . . up, up, up. No one had asked Lolly what she wanted, but that was the rule of life. Parents did the deciding, and children were decided about. *Go to sleep, Lolly*, her father had said at her door last night, and in a way she still felt as if she might be asleep and dreaming. But, of course, she wasn't.

The swing carried Lolly up again. *I'm going to be a Fortune again, and I'm taking you with me*, her mother had said. Did that mean she would have the name Fortune from now on?

As Lolly swung, she felt herself becoming strong and bold. She was turning into her secret-swing self, Lorelei Fortune, the girl who rode the wild horse of the air. Though Lolly was always called Lolly, she had actually been christened Lorelei, so both names were really hers. But Lolly Bancroft and Lorelei Fortune were like different people. Lolly felt afraid of doing the wrong thing, but Lorelei was always adventurous and brave. If only Lolly could walk away from the swing, carrying Lorelei inside her!

Up went the swing, and then down. Down, and then up again. Lolly had eleven cousins in town, but not one of them was a Bancroft. Every single cousin was a Fortune cousin. Only Lolly had missed out on that lucky lighthearted name.

The Fortunes believed they were the greatest family in the world. They stuck together and entertained one another. They celebrated one another's birthdays, had barbecues in one another's backyards, and sang loud, old family songs. Lolly's father, Ivor, watched, smiling politely, but he couldn't join in. He did not know the words and never bothered to learn. As for Lolly's Fortune cousins, they sang, too, or played hide-and-seek in darkening gardens. But, though Lolly went to all the Fortune parties, her cousins almost never came to visit her. Somehow, the lawns and garden around Lolly's house were too grand for all the trampling and scuffling of a Fortune get-together.

"You think you're too good for us," one cousin, Tessa, once said to Lolly. And another cousin, Tracey, had added, "Your Dad thinks he's so great because he's rich. Anyhow, you're not a proper Fortune—not like we are. You haven't got the name."

Uncle Toby Fortune and his family had come home to Fairfield only six weeks ago, but Pete, the second boy of that new family, was already a member of the gang who met in a treehouse in the forest behind Grandpa Fortune's house. Lolly had lived in Fairfield all her life, but she was still not a member of the gang.

"It's not just a gang. It's a sort of Fortune Investment Society really," Tessa would say. "Only we keep on spending our profit."

Gang or society, Lolly longed to join in, but no Bancroft could belong to a society (or gang) called the Good Fortunes Gang. And, somehow, to make things worse, Lolly wasn't even a particularly good

Bancroft. Honoria was always pointing it out, making Ivor even more anxious about her than he already was.

"You were born with two left feet, Lolly," he would say, and then he'd sigh and shake his head. When he sighed like that, Lolly wanted to draw herself up and give him a fiery glance.

"Lolly?" she wanted to say to him. "Lolly's a wet, half-chewed, sugary name. My name is Lorelei Fortune."

"My name is Lorelei Fortune," Lolly muttered, just to hear how proud and brave it sounded. "How can you sneak away in the night to Honoria?" she asked Ivor, though he wasn't there. "Come home at once and things will be all right again. Even better." The swing swept up so high that she felt she was being swallowed by the sky. "Much, much better. Things don't have to be the same as they always were. They can get better." But she could only say that because her father wasn't actually listening.

Then her mother called. She had to get off the swing. Dragging her feet along the ground to slow down, Lorelei felt herself coming back to earth again, though earth was much more uncertain at that moment than the swing. Somehow, her every-

day school shoes tied her to the ground. She was Lolly again. She turned around. Lorna was leaning over the veranda, smiling. But the fatherless house behind her seemed suddenly as strange and scary as an unknown forest in a fairy tale.

CHAPTER 3

The Fortune cousins had always gone to the state school, Fairfield Primary, but Lolly went to St. Joseph's Convent.

"After all, she *is* a Bancroft," said Honoria, talking over Lolly's head as usual. "Say what you like, there's a rough element at the state school."

When Honoria talked about a *rough element*, it was a way of mentioning the Fortune cousins without actually naming them. Honoria did not like the Fortune family, and sometimes behaved as if she thought Lolly had got her Bancroft blood through wicked trickery.

"Private schools do give that little extra polish. And we *all* agree that Lolly could do with a little polishing," said Honoria. "I know her father thinks so."

Getting her ready for her school polishing, Lorna brushed and plaited Lolly's fairish-brownish hair, smiled into her bluish-greenish eyes, and hugged her, growling and pretending to bite her like a kind and loving bear.

"Lolly . . . none of this is your fault."

"I know," said Lolly. "But life must go on."

"Right!" said Lorna. "Now, it's school. Bag! Bike! Big kiss for mother. Be good, and off you go."

All day at school, Lolly had that crumbly feeling. She sat behind her solid desk, with initials of St. Joseph's pupils from last year and the year before scratched into it. Lolly watched her writing hand, and imagined her pen, and then the fingers holding it, beginning to powder and drift down on to the paper like dust. Later, when she was making an owl mask for her part in a school play, it seemed as if her eyes were watching someone else's hands draw the feathers.

I'm here but I'm *not* here, thought Lolly. She put on the owl mask and looked through the owl eyes. But, behind the mask, her face felt as if it were smoothing itself out, becoming quite blank, like an egg. She quickly took the mask off again.

That afternoon, when school was over, Lolly put her bag on her bike rack, and her owl mask in the basket on the front. The mask stared up at her, looking rather frightening. She turned it facedown. Then, instead of biking straight home as she usually did, Lolly set off in the opposite direction. She went down Hill Street, through the little Hill Street Park, and into dangerous territory. She waited by the park gate as kids from the state school went by.

There, far down the street, came her cousins, Trace the Ace and her younger brother, Jackson, both on their skateboards. Even from a distance Lolly could see how cool Tracey looked, gliding serenely towards her, skillfully jumping the skateboard over uneven places in the footpath, swinging out around two other children who were merely walking. Tracey's pale hair flashed like a distant signal. Funnily enough, from a distance she reminded Lolly of Ivor, driving through Fairfield traffic in his Jaguar car. Once behind the wheel of his car, he stopped looking anxious, and became serene, as if he were gliding across all the troubles of the world.

Two boys, swinging their packs at one another by the park gate, stopped when they noticed a convent blazer. They put on posh voices and began to walk with mincing steps.

"Convent cats, Stink like rats!" they sang to each other. There was a rule that that was what the state school said to the private school. The boys waited, grinning, for her to shout back at them. Lolly knew she should reply with a well-known rude rhyme about the state school, but the words turned dusty in her mouth. Over the years, Honoria had somehow managed to turn Lolly into a whisperer, and there's not much point in whispering a rude rhyme. However, the boys thought her silence meant that she really did believe she was better than they were.

"You're spying on us, convent cat," one of them growled, his grin fading.

Just when it seemed the boys might actually do some serious bullying, there was a rush of wheels. Tracey was upon them.

"Leave her alone, creeps!" she shouted. "If you touch her, the whole Fortune family will gang up on you, and that means *me*, Trace the Ace!"

"We weren't going to touch her," said one of the boys. They hurried out of Tracey's reach. Tra-

cey spun her skateboard on its back wheels. Jackson copied her.

"What are you doing here, Lollipop?" Tracey demanded scornfully. "Convent cats get killed here. Their skins are hanging from fences all down this street. Go back where it's safe!"

"I was looking for you," said Lolly. "I have something to tell you."

"Go on, then," said Tracey impatiently. "Tell us!"

"What, what-what-what-what-what?" muttered Jackson strumming, then drumming the air. Watching Jackson was like watching an entire band riding on a single skateboard.

"I think I'm going to be a Fortune, too," Lolly said. "I mean, *really* a Fortune. I think I'm going to be *called* Fortune—like you."

"How?" asked Tracey. She looked interested. "Is Uncle Ivor changing his name? Cool move!"

"No," said Lolly. "Mother and Dad are separating."

"Real Fortunes don't get separated," said Tracey, sounding as if she were stating a universal rule —like the law of gravity. "They mate for life, like weasels. Is it weasels?" she asked Jackson. "You know . . . on that nature thing on television, it said that *something* mated for life."

"Swans and geese," said Jackson, dancing a little. He could actually dance on a skateboard. "But what about Prue?"

Prue was Tessa's big sister. She had already been married and had a baby. Now she was divorced. All this had happened to Prue before she was twenty.

"It was weasels," said Tracey. "Anyhow, Prue doesn't count. They just made her get married because she was having a baby. None of us were invited. But real Fortune marriages, which everyone's invited to, stick like superglue."

"But Lolly isn't a real Fortune," said Jackson. He turned to her. "You don't know the words, man. You haven't got the action, man." He called everybody "man," even the Fortune babies.

"Are your parents really splitting?" asked Tracey.

Lolly nodded, hunching her shoulders. She shivered slightly.

"They had a big fight last night," she said.

"Well, tell Lorna she can get half the house and half the Jaguar," said Tracey. "That's the law. She's allowed to get half of all that Bancroft stuff. Don't let him con her out of the Jag."

"He's already got it," Lolly said. "It *is* his car. I mean, he's allowed to have what he loves most."

Tracey looked grim.

"Okay, then why doesn't he have you?" she asked. "My father sells cars, but he doesn't sell us."

"Mothers get the kids and fathers get the cars," Jackson sang. "That's the law of nature from Mercury to Mars." He was quick with rhymes, and thought he might be a rap singer one day.

"Giving up the Jag!" cried Tracey, looking suddenly horrified. "Hey, I'm going to check up on your rights with Sharon Bluett. Her Mum's been divorced *twice*." She began to glide off, with Jackson following her. "If anything else happens, get on the phone and let us know," she called over her shoulder. Then she stopped, tilted the skateboard with her back foot, and spun it around so that she was facing Lolly again. "Hang in there," she called. Spinning around a second time, she glided off without saying a proper good-bye. Lolly stared after her.

She had not expected Tracey to be sympathetic. Tracey was never sympathetic. But it came as a shock to find Tracey was more worried about the Jaguar than anything else. The world around Lolly seemed to crumble a little more. She had to find a safe place quickly, or she would crumble, too. She decided to visit another cousin, Tessa.

CHAPTER 4

Tessa's sister, pretty Prudence, was warming a baby's bottle in the kitchen and talking to her boyfriend, Christopher Moody. As usual, Prudence was wearing weird clothes . . . a very short dress which seemed to be made of purple sacking with coffee-colored lace sewn around the bottom, and tights she had painted with smiling silver skulls and red toothbrushes.

"Prudence Fortune has ruined her life," Honoria used to say, looking pleased. However, for someone with a ruined life, Prudence seemed extremely cheerful. Her baby daughter was sitting on the floor in a jumpsuit which Prudence had painted with golden birds.

"Lolly Bancroft!" said Prudence, smiling. "What are you doing in *this* part of town?"

"Is Tessa here?" Lolly asked in her soft, Lollyish voice.

"In her room, reading up on interest rates," said Prudence. Lolly did not know for certain which room belonged to Tessa. She and her cousins mostly met at Grandpa Fortune's house.

When she did find her, Tessa really was checking interest rates. She had spread the financial pages of the paper all over the floor, and had outlined some of the figures in red.

"Hey!" she said, looking at Lolly in amazement. "What are *you* doing here?"

She was surprised in the same way that Tracey had been surprised, because Lolly had never come looking for her before. But Tessa was glad to have company, and immediately began to talk.

"I'm going to make an investment," she cried. "I've got to make sure I get the best interest, but some places only want your money if you've got five thousand dollars."

"I've got something to tell you," said Lolly. "I'm going to be a true Fortune, after all. I mean my name's going to be changed to Fortune."

"Hey! Why?" asked Tessa, staring.

"My parents are separating. They had this great

fight," said Lolly. "Mother hit Daddy with Honoria's . . . with Grandmother Bancroft's picture."

"Gosh!" exclaimed Tessa. "Your mother's getting divorced from a *Bancroft?*" She ran to the door. "Prue . . . hey, Prue! You're not going to be the only divorced one in the Fortune family. Auntie Lorna's getting a divorce . . . she's getting a divorce from a *Bancroft.*" The news echoed through the entire house.

"What?" yelled two voices. Feet hurried towards them from two directions. The first one through the door was not Prudence but Auntie Marama.

"Lolly," she said, "what did you say? Is Lorna actually getting a divorce?"

Lolly had not imagined telling anyone except Tessa.

"They had a fight," Tessa was shouting. "Auntie Lorna hit Uncle Ivor with an oil painting of old lady Bancroft."

"A photograph," whispered Lolly, but Tessa was making up her own story.

"A Fortune is divorcing a Bancroft," Tessa went on. "No one else would divorce a *Bancroft.* Everyone else would suck up to them because they're rich. But we divorce them."

"Oh, Lolly . . . how awful," said Aunt

Marama, giving Lolly a kind look. "Oh, I am *so* sorry. . . ." She hugged Lolly. Tessa paused, looking suddenly unsure of herself.

"We're sorry but *interested*," said Prudence. "Don't worry, Lolly, I'll bet you anything they get back together again. I reckon Ivor's crazy about Lorna."

Tessa stopped looking unsure, and began shouting again. "Christopher, did you hear that? A Fortune is divorcing a Bancroft."

"Shut *up*," said Aunty Marama, grabbing Tessa's shoulder and shaking her.

But Prue only grinned. She winked at Tessa and Lolly as she and her mother quickly set off to the kitchen to distract Christopher from brooding about divorce instead of thinking of marrying Prue.

Tessa sighed, as if the excitement was all over, and looked back, a little wistfully, at the financial columns of the newspaper.

"Do you know what?" she said. "I have saved up . . . one hundred dollars. *One hundred dollars!*" she repeated in a hushed, religious voice. "I've just got a bank statement. One hundred dollars. Actually, one hundred and three dollars! It's nothing to do with the cousins. They spend all their capital. This is all my own money. I've saved up pocket money, I've done baby-sitting for Prue, I've even done *gardening*, and I didn't spend one single solitary cent of my birthday money! I saved it all! And my bank statement came in the post today, and I have got . . . wait for it . . . I have *one hundred dollars*! Tah *dah*! And I want to invest it. Do you know about things like that? I mean Uncle Ivor manages a bank, so perhaps . . ."

Lolly was shaking her head. Tessa sighed.

"I started watching that money program on television," she said. "You know, the one that comes on just after the news."

"I don't watch that," Lolly said. "My father does . . . I mean he used to . . . I mean . . ."

"You have to keep watching it," Tessa explained, "and after a while you begin to understand it. And do you know what? Money's like a sort of game. I mean, it's serious, but like a video game, too. And if you're rich, you're the boss of the world."

"Well, at our school they say money doesn't buy happiness," Lolly said, but she could hear herself sounding uncertain.

"Well, I reckon it *helps*," said Tessa. "If I had money I'd get a Macintosh computer, and a horse, and a paddock to graze it in, and I reckon that would make me pretty happy. I was going to ask Uncle Ivor about investing and now he's gone—just when I need him. Blast!"

She looked over at Lolly, almost shyly.

"I've actually saved a hundred and three dollars," she said. "I've got three dollars of car-cleaning money in a vase in my room. Let's spend it. Let's go and get something to eat . . . not anything expensive, but three dollars' worth of something."

Lolly could see that Tessa was suddenly imagining what it must be like to have no father.

"Ice cream or chips?" she asked.

"Ice cream!" said Lolly.

Walking to a corner shop with Tessa, and choosing an ice cream a few minutes later, made the world seem almost solid again.

CHAPTER 5

"I don't know why you had to rush off and tell everyone else in the family," said Lorna.

They were sitting at the veranda table eating giant hamburgers, something they would never have done if Ivor had been at home. Out on the lawn, the swing was surrounded by a warm golden halo of late-afternoon sunshine.

"I wanted to tell the cousins that my name was going to be Fortune from now on," said Lolly.

"Oh, well, I don't know about *that*," said Lorna, looking flustered. "I hadn't thought quite as far ahead as that."

"You said you were going back to being a Fortune and taking me with you," said Lolly accusingly.

"Well . . ." Her mother looked a little bothered. "Well, I wish you'd waited a few days until . . . well, never mind," she said. "Did anyone ring while I was getting the hamburgers? Honoria? Your dad?"

"No!" said Lolly.

It was curious how much bigger the table on the veranda seemed with Ivor gone. It seemed to stretch for miles. Her father had a way of sitting at the table, staring into space as if he were seeing something more interesting in the distance. At such times he was there, but *not* there. Now, it was the other way around. He was *not* there, but there . . . there on the other side of the table where his space was . . . he was still invisibly watching them. Lolly tried not to look at his empty place.

The phone rang. Lorna got to her feet and walked casually through the glass doors that opened onto the veranda. Lolly could see her mother was trying not to run.

"This is Lorna Fortune," Lolly heard her say in a cool, elegant voice. Then there was a silence. "Lolly," she called, "it's for you. I think it's Tracey."

Tracey? thought Lolly. Tracey had never rung her before, but then they were both only just getting used to the idea of using the phone. Lolly and her mother passed each other in the doorway, Lorna coming out again, Lolly going in.

"This is Trace the Ace," said a voice in Lolly's ear. "Listen, you don't want to be a child of a broken home with no car, do you?"

"We've got my mother's car," said Lolly.

"But that's just an Escort," Tracey cried scornfully. "Dad sells hundreds of them . . . well, he sells a few, anyway. Listen, Lolly . . . *are* you listening?"

"Yes," said Lolly meekly.

"You tell your mother . . ." Trace paused. "Tell her that children from broken homes don't do well at school. And convents are cruel to them because the pope isn't into divorce. Tell her that. Are you listening?"

"Tracey!" Aunt Tiffany was yelling in the background. "Dinner's ready! Get *off* that phone!" Lolly could also hear the noise of small cousins quarreling and crying.

"I can't tell her that," murmured Lolly. "She'll worry."

"Make her worry," exclaimed Tracey. "She ought to worry. . . . All right! All right! I'm *coming*," she yelled at someone saying something be-

hind her. "Got to go now. Catch up with you later!" And she quickly hung up.

Lolly wandered back to the veranda. In one day she was not only a child of a broken home, but being given advice by Trace the Ace.

The phone rang again. Once again Lorna leaped up. However, once again the call was for Lolly.

"I think it's Tracey again," called Lorna rather crossly.

Lolly and her mother passed each other in the doorway, Lolly going in, Lorna going out. It was not Tracey. It was Tessa.

"Listen," she began. "Do you think Uncle Ivor would give me good investment advice now that he's getting divorced from us?"

"I think so," said Lolly doubtfully.

"Yes, but suppose he gives me bad advice out of revenge," said Tessa.

"I don't think he'd do that," said Lolly. "He likes giving good advice."

"Well, I've been thinking about it," Tessa went on, "and you know what? Hang on to him. Uncle Ivor, I mean. We haven't got another bank manager in the Fortune family. We're okay on second-hand cars, crane hire, and property deals, but we need a banker. Tell your mother."

"Tell her what?" Lolly asked. "Stay married to him because he's a bank manager?" She was surprised at her own voice. She sounded a little like Tracey. No! she sounded like Lorelei Fortune.

"Make it sound more sort of . . . romantic," said Tessa. "Hang on a minute!"

There was silence as Tessa tried to think of good, romantic things for Lolly to say to Lorna.

"Tell her your father's crazy about her," she said at last. "But don't tell her Prue said it. Just say everyone *knows*. And tell her to think of the family, stuck without good, free advice on investment."

Lorna was still sitting at the table, staring into space. How could she suddenly bring the conversation around to love and free advice on investment, Lolly wondered. The phone rang again.

"You get it this time," Lorna said. "Everyone wants to talk to you this evening, and nobody wants to talk to me."

Lolly went inside to answer the phone.

"Lorelei Fortune," she said in a cool, elegant voice, copying Lorna.

"Lolly, dear," said her father. He sounded tired and sad. He didn't sound irritable. "What sort of a day have you had?"

"I don't know," Lolly said. It was true. She

didn't quite know. The day had begun with invisible crumbling, yet the afternoon had somehow become filled with a sort of crazy excitement. Now, hearing her father's voice, Lolly wished he were safely at home—standing on his own mouse-gray carpet and grumbling about the bloodstains—instead of being on the other side of town with Honoria. She wanted to talk to him, to ask him something, but she didn't quite know what it was she wanted to ask.

"Dad," she began, but he interrupted her.

"Is Lorna there?"

"It's for you," Lolly shouted to her mother.

"About time, too," said Lorna.

They passed each other in the doorway, Lolly going out, Lorna going in.

"Hello," Lolly heard her say. Then she said, "I've got nothing to say to you," and hung up. Lolly stared at her mother, realizing Lorna had been waiting for Ivor to ring, just so that she could tell him she had nothing to say to him. It seemed like a fight at school.

As evening was falling over the garden, Lolly sat on the swing once more, swinging the sun down. Lorelei-Fortune thoughts rushed into her head and filled it to overflowing. What did her father think of all this? Lorelei Fortune wondered. Up she went, hanging for a dizzying, wonderful moment. Ask, she told herself. Is Prue right? Was Ivor really crazy about Lorna? It was easy to think about parents liking each other, but hard to imagine them crazy with love, like soap-opera people. Only yesterday, Lolly had heard Ivor complaining because the whole fridge smelled of fish soup. Do people complain about old fish soup to people they're crazy about? Ring Dad and ask him! Down she went, and then up once more. Yes! Ring him and ask him. Ask him if he wanted to be divorced. Tell him that she wanted him to come home again. Simple. It was a Lorelei-Fortune idea. Lolly carried it safely back across the lawn, up the veranda steps and into the house, and it actually seemed as if, this time, Lorelei Fortune left the swing and walked into the house with her.

CHAPTER 6

Lolly had wanted to talk to her father all day—but with no one else listening. She knew that if she rang him at work, he would be too busy to speak to her. There was nothing for it. She would have to ring him at her grandmother's house.

Lolly lay awake, waiting until her mother was in bed, and then ran softly downstairs and dialed Honoria's number. She imagined Ivor, unable to sleep, pacing backwards and forwards, missing Lolly, and crazy about Lorna—even though she sometimes left old fish soup at the back of the fridge. He might be longing to be telephoned and told he could come home again.

No such luck! It was Honoria who answered the phone.

"It's Lolly," said Lolly, and then corrected herself. "It's Lorelei. Could I talk to Dad, please?" She felt pleased with herself because she did not whisper.

"Your father's in bed, asleep," Honoria said. "I'm certainly not going to wake him. He's had a terrible day. Not that I'm going to get mixed up in any of this, Lolly, dear. I'm not going to let anyone turn me into a wicked mother-in-law."

Someone spoke in the background.

"You should be in bed, Lolly," Honoria said. It was her turn to whisper, or so it seemed to Lolly. "It's very late. Ring in the morning. Good night, dear." Then she hung up.

It must have been Ivor talking in the background, thought Lolly. So he was *not* in bed. Honoria just did not want her talking to him. But why not? Lolly stood there, frowning to herself. "She wants him back," murmured Lorelei Fortune, "but I'll bet he doesn't really want to be there. He can't want to live with Honoria more than he wants to live with us."

The telephone rang right beside her. Lolly leaped with the shock of its shrill cry. Ivor had rung back. He couldn't wait to speak to her! Spinning around quickly, Lolly accidentally knocked

the phone off the little table it stood on. Crouching, she grabbed the receiver.

"Lorelei Fortune," she said triumphantly. A voice was whispering on the other end of the phone.

"I can't hear," Lolly whispered back. Her father must be whispering so that Honoria wouldn't hear him.

"Did you tell her what I told you to tell her?" someone asked. It wasn't her father. It was Tracey. "What did she say?"

Lorelei Fortune invented quickly. "Mother said a lot of children come from broken homes and live happily ever after. She said it was better for me not to live with a lot of fighting going on."

"She got that from television," said Tracey indignantly. "I heard them saying that on that program about violence in the home."

A door opened noisily.

"What on earth's going on?" called Lorna. "Who's that on the phone?"

Lolly heard someone shouting at Tracey, too.

"She means it's better for *her*," Tracey said in a hurried mutter. "People say it's better for kids when they mean it's better for them. No sweat! We'll get them together again. My agent will be in touch with you." And once again she put the phone down quickly before Lolly had time to say anything more.

"It was Tracey again," Lolly told Lorna. "She was just ringing to see how I was."

"Tracey?" cried Lorna. "Three times in one evening!"

"Only twice," said Lolly. "It was Tessa, once. I think it's because I'm a Fortune now," Lolly added, even though she knew both her cousins really wanted her to go on being a Bancroft. Tracey liked having a Jaguar in the family. Tessa longed for good advice about investing her savings.

The following morning was a Saturday. The phone rang very early. Lorna got to it first this time, but once again the phone call was for Lolly, who was still in bed. She had never had so many phone calls before in her entire life. Lorna shouted for her, and stamped back to bed herself, grumbling that it was a bit rough to be woken so early on a Saturday morning. Lolly knew, from Lorna's expression, that the caller was not her father. She thought it would probably be Tracey again.

"I've got instructions to give you," said a strange voice.

"Who is it?" Lolly asked.

"Me," said the voice. "Me, Pete!"

It was Uncle Toby's second son, Pete Fortune, another member of the Good Fortunes Gang. "Tracey said I was to give you your instructions. Have you got a pen? You'll have to write them down."

"Yes," said Lolly in an efficient voice. Her father had been very strict about having pads and pens next to phones. She scribbled with the pen a little bit, but it knew immediately who was holding it and the ink would not flow.

"First, you tell your mother you want to go for a drive to the War Memorial Park after lunch. And then say that you want to walk on the track through the gardens," said Pete. "Got that? That's all."

"Why?" asked Lolly. Thank goodness she didn't need to write down those instructions.

"It's best if you don't know," said Pete. "Our gang is going to help you, but we're going to do it in a secret way so that if anyone asks you afterwards, you can say you didn't know anything about anything. Is your mother listening?"

"She's gone back to bed," said Lolly.

"If she says she will take you, tie a white handkerchief to your gate," Pete said. "A secret agent will bike past and check it out later in the morning." Lolly was sure he meant himself.

"You must learn the instructions by heart, and then swallow the paper. Good Fortunes signing off," said Pete, and hung up.

At least she didn't have to worry about swallowing the instructions. Lolly felt glad that the pen hadn't written for her.

She stared at the phone. Then, glancing rather guiltily at Lorna's closed door, she picked up the receiver again. She dialed her grandmother's number, shut her eyes and prayed that this time it would be her father who answered the phone.

But once again the voice that answered was Honoria's.

"Lolly, dear," she said, "I'm afraid your father's just gone to work. You know him . . . he's so conscientious, even on a Saturday morning. Goodness knows why. No one thanks him for it."

There was nothing for Lolly to do but plan to ring again later.

CHAPTER 7

Rather to Lolly's surprise, Lorna agreed quite cheerfully to the suggestion that they go for a drive in the early afternoon. Lolly could not find a white handkerchief to tie on the gate, but she hung a pale yellow one on a spike. A good agent would understand. Later, she and Lorna climbed into the Escort and drove slowly through Fairfield.

"It's a nice town," Lorna said. "I don't see what Honoria's got to complain about. Shall we call in on the Grandys?" She meant her parents, Grandpa and Grandma Fortune.

"On the way back," Lolly said quickly. She loved the Grandys, but once there, Lorna might settle down with a cup of tea, and begin explaining herself. It could go on for hours. Lorelei Fortune, down from the swing, and looking at everything through Lolly's eyes, did not want to wait around patiently. She wanted action.

It was a beautiful sunny day. The narrow road zigzagged up to the War Memorial and ended there in a paved circle, the memorial set in the middle of it. You could look out over the whole of Fairfield from here—over the shops, over the river, and out to sea. You could see the islands on the horizon.

The memorial stuck up into the sky like a stone finger asking for silence . . . a stone finger with a pointed nail. At night it might bend a little and scratch at the stars. Down the front of the stone finger ran a list of names, all names of Fairfield men and boys who had died in wars on the other side of the world. There were the names of two Fortunes among them, a great uncle of Lolly's, and, higher up, a great-great uncle. There were no Bancroft names, but that was because the Bancrofts had not been living in Fairfield in those days. Lorna stared out at the distant islands, looking thoughtful, even sad. From behind a phone box at the edge of the paved circle, Tracey and Jackson appeared. They grinned and waved at Lolly, pointing at a track into the park before ducking down again.

"Let's go for a walk," said Lolly.

They left the Escort parked in the stone circle, and wandered off along the track into the park. A hilltop wind came romping to meet them and kept them company all the way.

"You can't blame your father altogether," Lorna began suddenly, as if it were Lolly blaming him. Then she talked about how hard it had been for Ivor being an only child, and how Honoria had not wanted him to leave her and have a family of his own, and *of course* Honoria was lonely, but it was partly her own fault. She sneered at all Fairfield and all Fortunes. She refused to make friends. She had made life difficult for Lorna for years and years . . . not in any big way, but in dozens of little ways that were hard to complain about. Lolly knew all about Honoria's little ways. She thought about the night before, and the way Honoria had pretended Ivor was asleep and couldn't come to the phone. She glanced back over her shoulder.

"Why do you keep looking over your shoulder?" Lorna asked curiously. Lolly did not realize until then that she had been looking behind her. She couldn't tell Lorna that it was because a good Fortune plan was about to swing into action. It might come from any direction at any moment.

"It's time we went home, anyway," Lorna said. "Tracey has probably been trying to ring you all afternoon."

They reached the car and Lorna started the engine. But, when they were halfway down the zigzag hill, Lolly saw her mother grow suddenly worried. A moment later she pulled into a passing bay on the side of the road, slid out, and walked around the car. Then she came back looking cross.

"A flat tire," she said. "What on earth do I do now?"

"Can't you fix it?" asked Lolly.

"Of course I can. I've got the jack, the wheel brace, a spare tire . . . everything I need," her mother said. "But it's so awkward here. The road's so narrow. Look . . . that tire's absolutely flat. The tube must have burst or something." She smiled at Lolly. "Don't look scared. It's a nuisance, but no big deal, really."

Lolly was not looking scared because of the flat tire. Behind her mother she had caught a glimpse of Pete, Tracey, and Jackson peering around the corner, then ducking back out of sight. She was just wondering how this could possibly be part of a Good Fortunes plan when Lorna exclaimed in horror. Lolly turned in time to see her mother leap into the drain on the side of the parking bay, and hide herself in some bushes. A moment later a noble car, almost too noble for the War Memorial road, came smoothly around one of the hairpin bends. It was the Bancroft Jaguar, and the driver was Lolly's father. He waved at Lolly. It was almost as if he were expecting to see her standing there, all alone, waiting for him to come and rescue her. He tried to squeeze the Jaguar into the bay beside the Escort. There was not enough room for it. Part of it stuck out into the road. Ivor shook his head and leaped out, looking efficient.

"Never mind," he said. "This won't take a moment. Where are the car keys? I need to open the trunk."

"I haven't got them," said Lolly.

"Do you mean your mother went off and left you like this?" asked Ivor. He spoke over Lolly's head, looking left, then looking right. Something had pleased him, but he was slightly puzzled, too. An ordinary car came up the road towards them. Ivor was opening the back of the Escort with a spare Escort key on his key ring. He stopped and held his breath as the ordinary car inched past the Jaguar.

"So your mother's *ditched* you," he remarked meaningfully. Lorelei Fortune seemed to drain away out of Lolly. She didn't know what to say.

"Gone," she stammered. "She's gone."

"Gone where?"

"Gone to get help," said Lolly, trying not to look at the ditch behind her.

"Your mother can change a tire better than I can," Ivor said scornfully. "What's she playing at?" All the same he still looked quite pleased. He jacked the car up, took the wheel off, and put the spare wheel on in its place. It took about ten minutes and that included breath-holding time as other cars inched by the Jaguar. Lolly kept getting glimpses of Tracey and Jackson, first at the corner itself, then on the top of the bank that loomed over the corner. *Now*, she thought, *now* was the time to talk to her father. *Now* was the time to ask him if he really wanted to live with Honoria. *Now* was the time to tell him that she had tried to ring him twice. *Tell him now*, Lorelei Fortune said. *He's changing a tire*, Lolly answered, hesitating. *Now*, Lorelei commanded her.

"Dad," Lolly began firmly, "I want to ask you something. . . ."

"Just a moment," he said, working at the jack

again. The car sank down easily onto its new, hard tire.

Ivor straightened and looked around, frowning.

Lolly took a deep breath.

"Dad," she began again in a Lorelei Fortune voice. But she could see he still wasn't listening properly. Instead, he looked scornfully at the bushes that hid the drain. "Your mother must be feeling remarkably *guilty* about something," he said. "I mean, to ring me and then run away."

The bushes burst apart. Lorna sprang out, her hair full of leaves and twigs.

"I'm here," she said. "What a despicable thing to do. . . ."

"What do you mean?" Ivor cried.

"Don't deny it," she cried back. "You let the air out of my tire so you could come gliding by, accidentally-on-purpose, and I'm supposed to be *grateful* to you. But I could have changed that tire standing on my head."

"I know you could," said Ivor. "So why did you ring me up pretending to be Lolly. Of course I knew it wasn't Lolly!"

"Me? Me ring you?" screamed Lolly's mother.

Lolly opened her mouth. She could see Tracey and Jackson standing on the bank above the phone booth, staring over at them, and suddenly Tessa and Pete appeared, too. The whole Good Fortunes Gang was listening.

There was a sudden roar in the air. A big, rusty car skidded sideways around the corner, its tires slipping on the narrow road. It was filled with big kids from the Fairfield High School . . . six or seven teenagers of all colors. Ivor did not even notice them. The only thing he could hear was the sound of his argument with Lorna.

"Come on! Admit it. You watched us. Then you followed us," Lorna was yelling at him. "And while we were walking, you let the air out of my tire." She gestured dramatically up the road towards the War Memorial.

"Never! I don't *do* childish things like that. You rang me at the office. You talked in a high voice and pretended to be Lolly, and said you needed help," Ivor declared. "And here I am. So what's it all about? Why did you hide?"

"I hid because I didn't want to talk to you," Lorna shouted.

There was a dreadful, scraping sound. Ivor spun around as the rusty car accelerated, skidded, and vanished around the corner.

Ivor behaved in a way Lolly had never seen

him behave before. He howled like a werewolf, then took off after the rusty car, though he must have known he had no hope of catching it.

"Quick!" cried Lorna, and pushed Lolly towards their own car.

"But, Mother . . ."

"Quick! Don't argue!"

Lolly stared desperately towards Ivor, who had stopped running and was standing in the center of the War Memorial road with his back to them. There was no sign of the Good Fortunes Gang. The four cousins had faded into the trees on either side of the road. Lolly imagined them running off along the tracks of the War Memorial Park, much faster than members of most gangs or investment societies could run.

Lorna had opened the passenger door of the Escort. Now she pushed Lolly through it. Slamming the door, she sprinted around to the driver's side. Ivor turned.

"Wait, Lorna!" he shouted. "Just wait a moment, will you?"

But Lorna was already in the driver's seat. Ivor began to run back down the hill.

"Wait!" he shouted again.

The Escort roared into life. Lorna did some

inching of her own. The Escort tilted as she edged out of the bay and past the scraped Jaguar. Lolly gasped. But they were through. Off they went, leaving Ivor behind them. Perhaps it was only Lolly who heard his last cry.

"If *you* didn't ring me, who did?"

CHAPTER 8

"Tracey thought that if your mother saw the Jaguar she would be sorry she was separated from your father," said Pete to Lolly on the phone that evening. "She unscrewed the cap from your mother's tire and held the valve open with a nail."

"She was lucky to find a nail," said Lolly.

"She brought it with her," said Pete. "It has to be the right size."

"Dinner, Lolly!" called her mother. Lolly told Pete she had to go. In spite of the disastrous day, Lorna was looking cheerful.

"Poor Ivor," she said as they sat down at the dining-room table. "He loves that car of his. But what a trick to play on us! He must be desperate." She smiled happily.

Lolly, though, was not so sure. Two whole days had gone by since her father had left home. The world was beginning to feel less crumbly. She must be getting used to a house without him. Tomorrow morning, Lolly vowed, she would talk to Ivor properly. Even Honoria would not be able to stop her.

The next morning was Sunday. Lolly got up very early, and invented a breakfast for herself. She felt fearless and slightly wicked, stealing the scraps and putting them side by side on one big plate. She enjoyed one cold sausage, two kinds of cheese, three slices of salami, four chocolate biscuits, and an ice cream. Ice cream for breakfast was a Lorelei-Fortune idea. Then she went out and got Sunday off to a good start with some swinging. In its way swinging was like a sort of war dance.

It was going to be another beautiful day. The early sun could not quite reach the swing, because of the Bancroft brick wall. However, the top branches of the swing-tree were fiery with new light. Swinging, Lolly tilted her head back, and looked into crisscross twigs, growing and glowing above her. Suddenly dizzy in a wonderful way, with the rush of the swing and the light in the branches, she knew that *now* was the right time. No more telephoning. There had been too much of that already. She would get on her bike, ride around to her grandmother's house, and lurk among the hydrangeas in the garden until she saw her father on his own. Then she would leap out of hiding, and ask him things. Was he really crazy about Lorna? Did he really want to live with Honoria? And why did he seem to take Honoria's side so often, instead of Lolly's and Lorna's?

At that hour on a Sunday morning the streets were empty. The morning light made them strange and beautiful. Lolly, on the bike, was almost like Lorelei Fortune on her wild horse of the air. She was careful, and yet she rode more swiftly than usual, feeling she was the only moving Fortune in Fairfield, perhaps the only moving person in the world. From the basket of the bike, her owl-mask looked up at her. She had forgotten to finish it, but it still looked really good, Lolly thought. Its round, empty eyes stared out of carefully drawn feathers. Its open beak, drawn sideways, was fierce and sharp. She stopped outside an empty timber yard and put it on. This time her face behind it did not feel like a peeled egg. It felt suddenly wise. Wearing the mask, she was freer and wilder than she had ever been before. A fierce owl-faced girl was riding through Fairfield to talk to her father—to rescue him! Ivor needed rescuing.

Lolly padlocked her bike to a telegraph pole a little way down the road from Honoria's house. She could see her grandmother's gate was padlocked too, but that morning, Lolly was also Lorelei Fortune. Without hesitating, she climbed over the wall, grazing her knee painfully as she did so. Tracey would have gone over a wall without grazing anything, but Lolly hadn't had much practice wall climbing . . . not yet. On her hands and knees, the owl mask catching on all sorts of twigs, she crawled through the hydrangeas. There, framed in wide green leaves, was the front door of her grandmother's house. Ivor's Jaguar was drawn up waiting for a driver, its poor, scraped door turned towards her.

As Lolly watched, her father came out and put a folded rug and a basket onto the backseat of the Jaguar. Then he went inside again. Early as it was, she had caught him in the act of setting out somewhere. Lolly's luck was in at last.

She darted across the strip of lawn which had been cut into perfect neatness, opened the scraped door and scrambled onto the floor behind the front seats. When her father came back, Lorelei Fortune would be waiting for him.

But a moment later, she heard Honoria's cool, bleating voice—her words growing louder and louder as she came closer and closer. Lolly crammed herself down behind the driver's seat, her legs stretched out behind the passenger seat. She would not come out again until they were on the road, with Honoria well behind them. Then she would leap up and say, "Hi, Dad!"—just as cool as Tracey or Jackson.

But the door on the passenger side opened. Wherever her father was going, Honoria was going too. Her grandmother climbed neatly and carefully into the passenger seat.

"Stop worrying!" Honoria was saying. "She'll get over it. Of course, she will. The Fortunes might be a little common, but they have plenty of common sense. And if she doesn't . . . well, dear, I hate to say this, but it just could be a blessed release."

As she spoke, she pulled the seat belt across her chest. Her thin, wrinkled right hand began feeling for the slot between the two front seats. If she turns, Lolly thought, she'll see me. She imagined herself taking that searching hand and guid-

ing it in the right direction. It crawled backwards like a crab. Its fingers twitched and tapped within inches of Lolly's knee. Then they twitched and tapped forward, and found what they were searching for. There was a click. The seat belt was fastened, and Honoria had not turned around once. She had not even looked down.

Both seats sighed and shifted as Honoria and Ivor leaned back. The car started and moved off with its secret owl-girl hidden behind the driver's seat.

CHAPTER
9

"A day at the beach will clear your mind," Hono-ria said. "Don't ring Lorna! Don't run after her. Don't even think about her."

The car sped smoothly along. Suddenly, Lolly felt almost as if she were on the swing. Because she couldn't see out of the car window, she felt she was flowing along. Though she was in her own father's car, he did not know she was there. Her mother did not know where she was. Her cousins did not know where she was. Nobody knew where she was except Lolly herself. Telegraph wires gently looped past in long shallow curves. No wonder she was reminded of the swing! Up, down, and then up again. Sometimes it seemed as if the wires were actually flying, swooping gracefully along beside them.

"Mind you," said Honoria, leaning back firmly, "I did warn you before you married. . . ."

"I don't want to talk about it," said Lolly's father. "You just can't be fair to Lorna, Mother, and she can't be fair to you."

"Oh, so it's *my* fault, is it?" said Honoria. She gave a little laugh. "I might have guessed it would come to that."

"It's my fault," Ivor said quickly. "I *am* finicky. I complain a lot. I'm always nagging at Lolly, for example. . . ."

"There's plenty to nag at," said Honoria quickly. "It's for her own good, dear. At least *I* understand that. There's a rough element in the Fortune family. You don't want her copying them."

"Let's forget it," said Ivor. "It's a lovely day. Let's enjoy it, if we can."

"There's more to marriage than a pretty face," Honoria went on as if he had not spoken.

"I've been married twelve years. I know that," said Ivor. "Ma, don't go on about it, or I'll turn back to town."

Honoria then began to talk about something else. She had a gentle voice, but as it went on and on and on, Lolly began to feel sorry for her father. Honoria said Ivor was all she had, so she couldn't help taking an interest in his life. She was so proud of him. He had done so well. She wanted to help him. She couldn't help getting angry when she thought he wasn't appreciated.

Lolly stuck out her tongue at the back of the car seat.

"Lorna will see reason," said Honoria. "Those Fortunes never give up a dollar if they can avoid it."

"Ma," said Lolly's father, sounding tired. "What's the use of taking a break from my troubles if you talk about them all the time?"

"Was I?" asked Honoria innocently. "I suppose it's so much on my mind. I can't help feeling for you, after all you've done for them."

"Let's stop and have a cup of tea, shall we?" asked Lolly's father.

The car swerved left then right.

"It doesn't look like much of a place," said Honoria.

"It's the best there is," said Lolly's father. Then they left the car.

Lolly waited a moment or two after they had gone. She wriggled around, working herself loose again, then very slowly peeped over the edge of the window. She saw the backs of her father and Honoria walking briskly towards a rather dilapidated general store. TEAS, said a notice outside it. Just as well I'm disguised, thought Lolly behind her owl mask.

She marched boldly into the shop. There her father and grandmother were, sitting at a table in the window looking completely annoyed with one another.

"A double ice cream," said Lolly loudly. She thought a loud voice would be a disguise for someone who often whispered. Neither her father or her grandmother looked at her.

"What flavor?" asked the man behind the counter.

"Chocolate ripple on the bottom and hokey pokey surprise on the top," Lolly answered.

"I thought it might be a holdup," said the man behind the counter, looking at her mask in an amused way.

"I have to be disguised," said Lolly. Then she carried the ice cream back to the car. Even Tracey couldn't have been so cool. No doubt about it, Lorelei Fortune was out and about in the world.

One thing she *was* certain of: her father was not enjoying life with Honoria.

Lolly scrambled into the back of the car and tucked herself and her ice cream down behind the passenger's seat this time, not the driver's seat. Just as she was finishing her ice cream, her father and her grandmother came back to the car. Once again, the thin fingers twitched close to Lolly's knees as the seat belt was fastened. Within another moment they were speeding on their way.

"I must say," said Honoria after a short silence, "you're not easy to sympathize with, Ivor."

"Look!" cried Lolly's father, "you were the one that said I should think about something else. Now you won't stop talking about it. And it's none of your business."

"Oh, so it's none of my business?" cried Lolly's grandmother. "Haven't I've done my best over the years? Haven't I been generous to Lorna, and perfectly sweet to the child?"

"What do you mean, the child?" cried Lolly's father. "Her name's Lolly. Call her by her name."

"Yes! Call me by my name!" Lolly's lips shaped the words. "My *real* name."

"Lolly, then," said Honoria. "I've always been sweet to Lolly, though it's not been easy. She's a plain little thing, and not too bright. Even you must admit that. She's not real Bancroft material, poor little Lolly."

But Lorelei Fortune was not plain or poor or little. She was brave and bold and beautiful behind her wise owl mask. She scrabbled as she bent her knees in the space between the front seats and the back one, pulling her feet in under her, quickly, not clumsily.

"What's that?" cried Honoria, feeling something struggling behind her as if it were battling upwards to space and light. Lolly unfolded like a tree, and stood over her.

"Stop calling me Lolly. I'm Lorelei Fortune," she cried. "And I *am* bright. I'm *blazing!*"

Glancing back, Honoria saw a fierce owl face glaring over her shoulder. She screamed with fear. Through the mask, for the first time in her life, Lorelei Fortune saw Honoria look terrified. It was a wonderful moment—like being high on the swing —and it seemed to pause as if it might last forever.

"Dad," she shouted. "Come home again! I want you at home."

CHAPTER 10

Ivor and Honoria could no longer have a picnic with stowaway-Lolly for company. They turned around and made for home again.

"I'm sorry to say this about a daughter of yours, dear," Honoria began, but Ivor stopped her.

"Don't say anything!" he exclaimed.

"Oh, I see," Honoria cried. "You're going to defend her, are you? After all I've done for you, you're going to let her frighten me out of my wits. She could have killed me, with my heart the way it is."

"Ma, please don't start all that again," begged Ivor. "You know Dr. Morton says you've got a heart like an elephant."

For some reason this made Honoria angrier

than anything Lolly could have said or done. She talked in a tight, furious voice, demanding apologies, and a punishment for Lolly. But then, when Ivor did not take any notice, she grew quieter and at last completely silent, staring out at the countryside as if there were nobody worth talking to in the car. Secretly triumphant, Lolly-Lorelei watched the power lines swinging by in thin, black waves.

When they reached Honoria's house, Lolly thought her grandmother would slam the Jaguar door and march inside without saying a word. Instead, she cried in a softer, more desperate voice than her earlier one, "Ivor, please! Don't make a fool of yourself again."

"Please don't be so cross, Ma," said Ivor. "It's bad for you. After I've taken this monster home, I'll catch up with you later."

His eyes met Lolly's in the rearview mirror, and to her surprise he winked at her. He wasn't good at winking, but it suddenly seemed to Lolly that he might improve with practice.

"Well, you certainly frightened the wits out of poor old Honoria," he remarked as they drove past the hydrangeas.

"I wanted to frighten her," Lolly said.

"You terrified both of us," said her father.

"I rang you twice," Lolly said, "but she wouldn't let me talk to you."

The car stopped outside Lolly's house. They sat together in the Jaguar, Lolly in the front seat now, beside her father. Her bicycle, shrouded in sacking to protect the Jaguar's upholstery, was slumped in the backseat. They were alone together at last.

"She's very lonely, you know," said Ivor Bancroft at last. "She was the most important person in my father's life. She wants to be the most important person in mine. She hates taking second place."

"Are we really important, Mother and me?" Lolly asked. She wanted to hear him say they were.

"Of course you are!"

There was the simple answer to her simple question.

"But your mother mightn't want to stay married to me," Ivor went on. "I worry too much to make a good Fortune."

"You're too disapproving," said Lolly. Ivor looked startled.

"Well, some things deserve to be disapproved of," he said.

"You disapprove of fun," said Lolly. "Of Fortune fun. You don't sing along."

"I *don't* disapprove of fun," Ivor cried. "But I'm just not a singer-alonger. I'm a listener. After all, singers need listeners, don't they?"

That was true, Lolly thought with surprise. She loved the Fortune family. She longed to be part of the Good Fortunes Gang, but her very best times were on her own, swinging in silence on the swing. Perhaps that's where Lorelei Fortune worked best, though it was nice to think she could come down from the swing whenever she was needed.

"Come in with me," Lolly said. "Come in and tell Mother that you want to stay married to her."

Ivor laughed.

"She already knows *that*," he said. "She's the one who has to make up *her* mind."

"I'll tell her I *want* you to stay married," Lolly said. "I really do. And I'll stop knocking over tea and bleeding on the carpet."

"Bleeding on the carpet?" Ivor sounded dismayed. "On the new gray carpet? Did you cut your foot on the broken glass?" Then he laughed a little, and shrugged. "How awful for you, but blood on the carpet doesn't matter . . . not compared with everything else," he said. "I'm sorry."

Lolly saw for the first time that he thought he might not be good enough for her, just as she thought she might not be good enough for him. She told a little lie . . . at least it seemed like a little lie. "You're just right," she said. Once she said it, she found she meant it.

Ivor did something Lolly was not expecting. He turned towards her and put his arms around her.

"Lolly, dear, you're just right, too," he said. "I'll learn to worry less. I learned commercial law. I must be able to learn other things as well."

"And will you tell Tessa how to invest her hundred dollars?" asked Lolly. She had explained to him how much the Good Fortunes Investment Society wanted to keep him in the Fortune family.

"Tessa should put her hundred dollars towards the cost of repairing the side of my Jaguar," said her father, letting Lolly go again. He took off his glasses and wiped them with his clean handkerchief. He always had a clean handkerchief. The remains of a tear was rolling down the side of his nose. "But tell her to come into the bank with her

hundred dollars and I'll advise her how to get the best interest. I didn't know she was so interested in investment, but you often miss out on important details in big family get-togethers. When everyone's singing along you don't hear solo voices, do you? Now, off you go to your mother. I'd better drive home and calm Honoria. You scared her out of her wits."

"I scared her out her wits with my too-whit too-whoo," said Lolly. She and Ivor looked at each other and suddenly burst out laughing at the thought of the fierce owl-girl rising up above Honoria and terrifying her.

"Well, off you go, Lorelei Fortune," said Ivor once more, this time with a sigh and a smile.

"You said I was more important than Honoria," argued Lorelei Fortune quickly. "Walk me in. Please, Dad!"

"But you have a mother and a Fortune family," Ivor said. "Honoria's only got me, Lolly."

"Call me Lorelei," she said, and for the first time she felt that from now on she would always be Lorelei, even to herself. "That's the name you chose for me. And, Dad, just drive up to the house. Don't stay outside like a visitor."

"All right, Lorelei!" said Ivor, starting the Jag-

uar. Its motor purred immediately like a good, obe-
dient cat. They turned in at the gateway in the
brick wall, drove past the swing-tree, and drew up
outside the veranda, just as Lorna came out to
meet them.

CHAPTER
11

The Good Fortunes Gang always met in a Fortune Family tree house in the middle of two acres of forest belonging to Lolly's Fortune grandparents. Grandpa Fortune was working in the garden as Lorelei biked through the gate at the foot of the hill.

"The others are up there already," he called, just as if he were used to seeing Lorelei arrive on her bicycle and climb the track into the bush. "Call in and say hello to us later."

Lorelei knew just where the tree house was, but the Fortune cousins were laughing and shouting so loudly that anyone could have found them. A rope with knots in it dangled down from the tree-house branch, and someone had nailed slats of wood onto the tree trunk, making a rough ladder.

Standing underneath the tree, she shouted, too.

"It's me!" she cried.

There was silence. For a second, she could hear a bellbird calling, far off among the trees. Then there was a scuffling sound. Tracey looked down from the tree house, then vanished again.

"It's Lolly," Lorelei heard her saying to the others. "Just because her name's Fortune now, she thinks she can join."

"My name's not Fortune," Lorelei shouted. It was funny that, when she was telling them her name was *not* Fortune, her words came out in a real Fortune yell. "And don't call me Lolly. From now on everyone's got to call me Lorelei, or I won't answer." That was another strange thing. It was her first name, not her last, that had been changed by the adventures of the past few days.

Tracey walked like a tightrope walker out onto one of the branches that supported the tree house. Jackson followed her so quickly it seemed they must be wired together.

"Make room!" commanded Tessa, who came next. Then the three of them had to shuffle a long way along the branch to let Pete come out of the tree house and stand beside them. Pete grinned at Lolly. He was the only one who was smiling.

"You said your name was going to be Fortune," Tracey said crossly. "Make up your mind!"

"I have made it up," Lorelei said. "My mother can go back to being Fortune if she likes, but I'm going to be called Bancroft. And Lorelei!"

"Hey! Have they made up, after all?" asked Tessa suddenly.

"Dad came home for a while last night, and I think Mother was pleased to see him," said Lorelei. "At any rate they had a cup of tea together, and they laughed twice, and I saw Mother pat him on his shoulder, and then my grandmother, Honoria, rang to find out where he was."

"Did he go back to old lady Bancroft?" asked Tracey scornfully. "What a wimp!"

"Mother *told* him to go," said Lorelei. "But she wasn't mad with him anymore. She was just a bit sorry for Honoria, because I'd jumped out at her and frightened her."

"Jumped out at her?" cried Tessa. "You? Why?"

"I'll tell you if you let me join the club," said Lolly cunningly.

"You can't join the club if you're not called Fortune," said Tracey.

"It's more fun to be a Fortune," said Jackson.

"Well, I'm making it fun to be a Bancroft," Lorelei cried boldly.

"Fun to be a Bancroft? How?" asked Tracey.

"Well, we could build a tree house in my swing-tree . . . a sort of *branch* meeting place, like you have branches of banks, but really in the branches," Lorelei said. "And we could have parties up there."

The Fortunes on the branch above looked at each other.

"Now you're here, you might as well come up," said Tracey. "Anyhow, cousins have to stick together whatever their names are."

"We'll be the Good Fortunes Gang *and* Investment Society, with a headquarters *and* a branch," said Pete, siding with everyone.

"Mind you, Fortune's still the best name to have," said Jackson.

"*Best* and *Bancroft* go better together," Lorelei said boldly, and, rather to her surprise, Tracey grinned, and punched Jackson's arm as if to say, Think about that, man! Then she stretched her hand down towards Lorelei, who had started to climb.

As she approached the branch, her left-hand fingers curled over the edge of the tree-house plat-

form, and her right-hand fingers wiggled in the air. Tracey's hand took hers. A moment later, Lorelei was sitting among the cousins, part of the gang at last.

It was wonderful to be there. Her mother and father were getting over their quarrel. She would go home and find them together again, she was sure. And her swing would be waiting for her, ready to carry her up into the air. But that was for later, when she would really enjoy being on her own. Now was the time for being one of the cousins and part of the Good Fortunes Gang up among the leaves.

ABOUT THE AUTHOR

Margaret Mahy is an internationally acclaimed storyteller who has twice won the British Library Association's Carnegie Medal and has received the (London) *Observer* Teenage Fiction Award. She has also won the Esther Glen Award of the New Zealand Library Association five times. Of her teenage novels published in the United States, *The Changeover* was a Best Book of the American Library Association and was the International Board on Books for Young People Honor Book in 1986. *Memory* was a *School Library Journal* Best Book and a *Boston Globe/Horn Book* Honor Book. She has written more than fifty books for young readers, including *The Good Fortunes Gang*, the first of four books detailing the adventures of the children of the extended Fortune family.